Religious School 14.95 12/98

Strudel, Strudel, Strudel

by STEVE SANFIELD   paintings by EMILY LISKER

ORCHARD BOOKS • NEW YORK

Text copyright © 1995 by Steve Sanfield
Illustrations copyright © 1995 by Emily Lisker

Orchard Books, 95 Madison Avenue, New York, NY 10016

Manufactured in the United States of America. Printed by Barton Press, Inc.
Bound by Horowitz/Rae. Book design by Mina Greenstein.
The text of this book is set in 15 point Bodoni. The illustrations are oil paint on canvas reproduced in full color.   10 9 8 7 6 5 4 3 2 1

Library of Congress Cataloging-in-Publication Data
Sanfield, Steve. Strudel, strudel, strudel / by Steve Sanfield ; paintings by Emily Lisker.
p.   cm. "A Richard Jackson book"—Half t.p.
Summary: Explains why teachers living in Chelm may not live on the top of a hill, own a trunk with wheels, nor eat apple strudel.
ISBN 0-531-06879-X.   ISBN 0-531-08729-8 (lib. bdg.)
[1. Jews—Folklore. 2. Chelm (Chelm, Poland)—Folklore. 3. Folklore—Europe, Eastern.]
I. Lisker, Emily, ill.   II. Title.   PZ8.1.S242St 1995 398.2′09438′402—dc20 [E] 94-24858

For the children of the San Juan Ridge—
then and now

—S.S.

To the city of Woonsocket
with affection

—E.L.

Chelm is just like any other town in the world except for two things.

The first is that Chelm is inhabited entirely by fools and simpletons who happen to think that they are all, each and every one of them, the wisest people in the entire world—which only goes to show that they are indeed a bunch of fools and simpletons.

For example, when a fire burned down a whole neighborhood one night, were the Chelmites angry or upset? Of course not! They thought the fire was a miracle. After all, they reasoned, were it not for the bright flames, which let them see the fire, how would they have been able to put it out on such a dark night and thus save the rest of the town?

Chelm is also set apart from other places by its signs. Only the Chelmites understand them.

In the Town Square on a post under two lanterns is a sign that says SEARCH HERE. To anyone but a Chelmite it makes no sense whatever, but to Chelmites it's as clear as the toes on their feet.

You see, there are few other lights on the streets of Chelm, so if you were to lose something at night in another part of town, it would be impossible to find it in the dark. Thus the sign, which strongly suggests you SEARCH HERE in the Town Square where there's plenty of light.

Then there's the large sign that's posted in front of the House of Study—

A TEACHER MAY NOT LIVE ON TOP OF A HILL
A TEACHER MAY NOT OWN A TRUNK WITH WHEELS
A TEACHER MAY NOT EAT APPLE STRUDEL

To understand this sign, it is necessary to look back through the years to the time when Chelm was a very young and a very poor village.

Zaynul was the schoolteacher back then. He was a kind and gentle teacher, and everyone in Chelm appreciated and respected him. But because Chelm was so poor and because teachers have never been paid well, Zaynul was not paid well either.

He and his wife, Zeitel, were able to scrape by, and each week they always seemed to have enough for the wine and candles they needed to welcome the Sabbath. Neither one ever complained—that is, until they developed a craving for apple strudel.

It came about in this way. Because he was so esteemed, Zaynul and his wife were invited to all the celebrations and special occasions in the lives of his students—births, Bar Mitzvahs, weddings. And at every celebration apple strudel was served.

In Chelm apple strudel was considered to be the delicacy of delicacies. *The food of angels,* people called it. It was expensive and difficult to make, with its delectable filling of apples and nuts and raisins, sugar and cinnamon, and bits of bright yellow lemon peel all rolled in a light golden dough.

The more Zaynul and Zeitel ate apple strudel, the more they wanted it. Of course, on Zaynul's meager salary it was impossible to buy all the necessary ingredients, so except for those special occasions they went without.

One winter night Zaynul awoke from a dream. As he lay there thinking about it, he heard Zeitel stirring beside him.

"Zeitel, my sweet, are you awake?" he asked.

"Yes," she answered. "I just had this lovely dream."

"What was it about?"

"Well, in my dream you and I were sitting at our kitchen table, and there in front of us were platters and platters of apple strudel. They were piled up like melons in the market, but just as I was about to take my first bite, I woke up. It was such a lovely idea."

"That's amazing, absolutely amazing," exclaimed Zaynul. "I had exactly the same dream, but just as I was about to take what I was sure would be the first of many wonderful bites, I, too, woke up. It's too bad real life can't be like our dreams."

They lay there in the dark, thinking their own thoughts, which happened to be about eating apple strudel, when suddenly Zeitel sat straight up in bed and declared, "I've got it. I've got it."

"The strudel?" asked Zaynul.

"No, silly, not the strudel, but I do know how we can have as much as we want."

"Well, what are you waiting for? Tell me quickly. My mouth is watering."

"We can't have it today, but if we follow my plan we'll be able to have as much as we want next spring."

"You mean there are going to be lots and lots of celebrations?" Zaynul asked, a little confused.

"No. I'm talking about a way we can buy apples and raisins and nuts and spices and even lemons, and then I'll be able to make all the apple strudel we can eat. Every week you and I will each put away a zloty, one zloty, and by the time spring arrives we'll have all that money for apple strudel."

"I always knew I was married to a woman as wise as King Solomon, but where will we put all those coins? We can't just leave them out where they might tempt even the kindest of thieves."

"You know the empty trunk my uncle left us, the one with wheels that sits by the door?" Zeitel asked. "We'll cut a small hole in the top, and each week we'll drop our coins in. Before long we'll have enough for strudel, strudel, and more strudel."

So a hole was cut in the trunk, and that Sabbath Zaynul and Zeitel each deposited a zloty—he before going off to synagogue to pray and she before lighting the Sabbath candles.

However, as the days passed, Zaynul began to think, always a dangerous occupation for a Chelmite. *Every week I give Zeitel all the money I earn except for a few coins. I never have enough for books or a bit of snuff, and now, dropping a zloty in the trunk will give me even less to not have enough with. Zeitel always seems to have enough for what we need. Surely she'll be able to save a zloty every week, and that should be plenty for our apple strudel.*

So Zaynul stopped dropping coins into the trunk.

At the same time, Zeitel was having her own thoughts, which were remarkably similar to those of her husband. *I have barely enough to buy what I need for our household. How am I going to be able to spare a zloty a week? Besides, my husband always does what he says he will, and his coins should be more than enough for our apple strudel.*

So Zeitel stopped dropping coins into the trunk.

Winter came and went with its cold and snow and ice, and then suddenly it was spring. The grass was knee-high, the leaves and the birds had returned to the trees, flowers bloomed, butterflies flitted, children skipped and sang, and Zeitel and Zaynul turned their thoughts to their feast of apple strudel.

"Zeitel, my sweet, now that spring is here, don't you think it's time to open your uncle's trunk? I'm getting a strong craving for you know what."

"Yes, my love," Zeitel responded. "I am, too. Soon we'll have all the apple strudel of our dreams."

"Strudel, strudel, strudel," Zaynul sang softly.

"Strudel, strudel, strudel," Zeitel joined in.

"Strudel, strudel, strudel," they sang together.

They lifted the lid. There in the bottom of the trunk lay two coins. Two coins. No more, no less. They stared in silence for a very long moment at those two lonely coins, and then Zaynul screamed, "We've been robbed."

"Thief, thief! A thief stole our strudel money," yelled Zeitel.

Husband and wife both moaned and wailed until a new idea entered Zeitel's mind. "Wait a minute. Wait a minute!" she insisted. "Why would a thief go to all the trouble of robbing us and then leave two coins behind?"

"Why indeed?" said Zaynul.

"There is no reason, no reason at all," Zeitel continued, "unless . . . Zaynul, tell me the truth. You haven't been putting in a zloty every week, have you?"

"Well, I . . . I . . . ," Zaynul stammered.

"The truth, Zaynul. Tell me the truth."

Zaynul could no more tell a lie than he could fly in the sky. "No, not since the first week, but I don't think you did either. If you had, there'd be enough for all the apple strudel we'd ever want."

"I was counting on you," Zeitel cried. "You said you would and you didn't."

"You said you would."

"You said you would."

And so it went, Zeitel screaming at Zaynul and Zaynul screaming back. The shouting grew louder. The arm waving grew wilder. The jumping up and down grew more frenzied. Zeitel lost her balance and fell headfirst into the trunk. Her legs stuck straight up, flapping as if each one had a life of its own. "Help. Help me," she pleaded.

Zaynul reached in and tried to pull her out. Instead, he got pulled in. They both thrashed about, this way and that, elbows and knees, arms and legs all jumbled up, and suddenly the lid slammed shut.

Now their thrashing really started in earnest. They yelled. They screamed. They moaned. They groaned. They pushed. They pulled. They bounced. They jounced.

All that hurly-burly set the trunk in motion. Slowly it began to move. First inch by inch out the front door and into the street. Once it reached the street, its small iron wheels started turning faster and faster as the trunk gained momentum and headed down the hill toward Market Square.

It was a sight that had never been seen before in Chelm—a large trunk rolling down the street alone with muffled cries and screams coming from inside.

The dogs were the first to notice. They began to bark and yelp. One, two, three, four dogs—large dogs, small dogs—every dog in town. All chasing the trunk. Their yipping and yelping and yapping caught the attention of the children, and they joined in the chase, delighted with this new game. Housewives poured from their houses, shopkeepers from their shops to see what all the excitement was about.

The procession of the rolling, moaning trunk followed by a mass of barking dogs, laughing children, and bewildered adults grew larger and larger as it picked up speed and drew closer and closer to Market Square at the bottom of the hill.

When the trunk crashed into Perl's pottery stall, it didn't even slow down. It knocked over the flimsy shelves, sending dishes and bowls and pots sailing in all directions.

As the trunk went flying past, men and women started screaming—some in fear, some in terror, some in confusion. All that noise startled the animals. Goats and cows and horses were panicked by the commotion. They pulled loose from their tethers and scattered, knocking over anything and everything.

The entire market was one huge mishmash. Melons rolled wherever they pleased. Hay wagons stood upside down. Chickens sat atop merchants' heads. Silk ribbons decorated a billy goat's horns. Everything was topsy-turvy. Everything was a shambles. The children loved it.

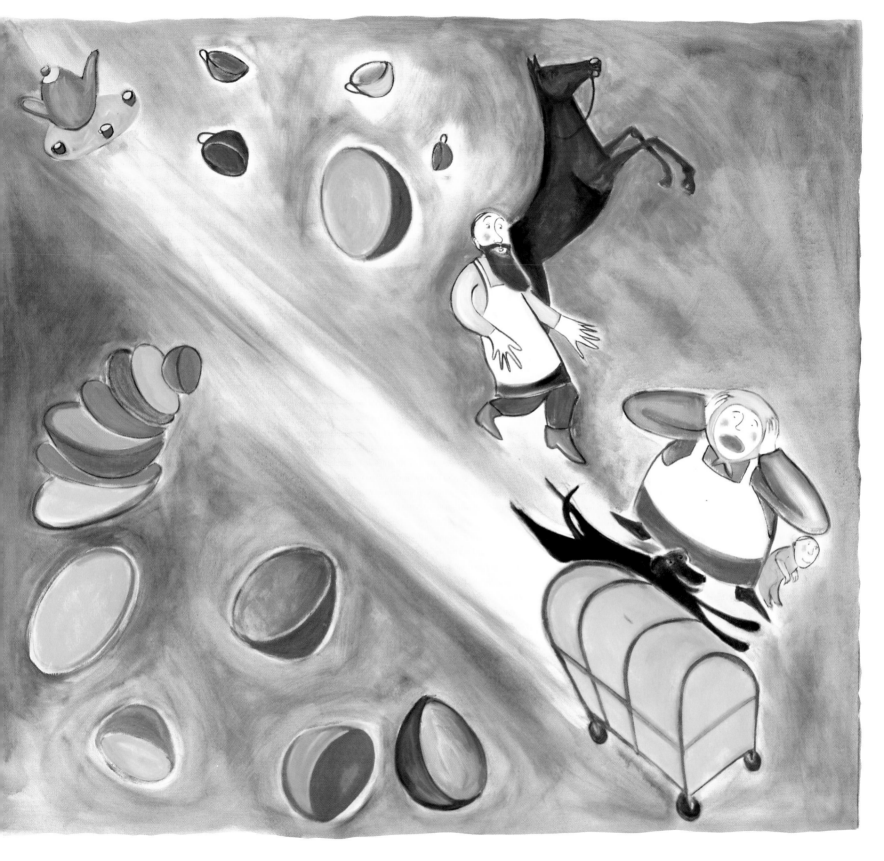

The rolling trunk gradually lost its momentum and finally came to rest against the water pump. It was smeared with broken eggs and flour and spilled milk, and all kinds of feathers were sticking out of the gooey mess.

The children stopped running. The dogs stopped barking. The merchants stopped yelling. Except for the occasional crowing of a confused rooster, the only sounds in the market were the muffled shouts and shrieks coming from inside the trunk.

"Demons," Tevye the Tinsmith called out. "There are demons in the trunk."

No one moved. Everyone seemed to be afraid—everyone except the children. They were having too much fun to worry about demons. They moved closer and listened.

"Help. Please help us," they heard.

"Let us out. Please."

Little Itzak, the cobbler's son, was the first to recognize the voices. "It's our teacher," he announced. "It's our teacher, Reb Zaynul."

A few of the men stepped forward and carefully opened the lid. There were Zaynul and Zeitel, their arms and legs and clothes all entangled. But once they were out of the trunk, they seemed no worse for their unplanned trip down Market Street.

When they finally explained what had happened to them, the Council of Seven Sages was called together for an emergency meeting. For seven days and seven nights they discussed, deliberated, and dissected the situation, and then they announced their decision.

They agreed that nothing like this had ever happened before and that, for the sake of the peace and harmony of the community, it should never be allowed to happen again. Therefore, from this day forward Zaynul and Zeitel would receive a honey cake each Sabbath. That way their sweet tooths would be satisfied, and there'd be no need for them to save their money for apple strudel.

And just to be absolutely certain that an incident like this would never, ever occur again, a large sign was posted in front of the House of Study that reads,

It's been that way in Chelm from that day to this, and now, just like every other Chelmite, you, too, understand what this sign means.